ISLAND'S WHISPER

SHORT STORIES BY: MELISSA I.EIGHTS

CONTENTS

INTRODUCTION

Just as how a painter feels when the paintbrush touches a canvas, that is the same feeling she gets when her fingers touch the keyboard. It is the same feeling that is felt when a bass guitar is a strum. Her soul comes alive, as every person has an art! Melissa I. Eights was born in Aruba. She enjoyed her days as a happy lark that looked forward to her evenings spent at the seashores with her older brother.

Life for them took a different turn when they migrated to Sint Maarten where both parents earned a better living and took up their posts. Her mother taught elementary school for many years. Her father was an administrative clerk by day and at night, a youth pastor.

During her teen years; Melissa was quite an individual who others thought to be quite strange! Despite this, she wore her label with pride and she moved to the United States where she began a study in Biology and ended in Business Administration.

Being far away from home was a dream come true. She welcomed the quest for freedom. To some spectators, they deemed this a mistake. To others, it was a great learning experience. This island girl journeyed from the night light to campus life and has found comfort in church life!

There were many unpleasant turns along the way. All of it has helped to mold her. She has lived! She has loved and is also a mother to an inquisitive 9-year-old son, was a daring wife to a carpenter, an educator, a toy creator, a puzzle maker, a daughter, a sister, a cousin, and an aunt.

She has self-published and her greatest wish would be for her to spend her days in the hills tapping away at her computer as an accomplished writer.

This prose has been written due to her love of literature and drama budding over the years. Pieces that have stood out have been Wuthering Heights, The Scarlet Letter, and finally, The Hills Were Joyful Together! This is only a fraction of the timeless pieces which has stood out. This has been a peep into the world of Caribbean prose!

#4 Oracabessa

St. Mary

Jamaica

West Indies

Thursday 21st May, 1990.

Dear Margo,

Today and tomorrow are holidays so I decided to take some time and catch up on some emailing and work. Well, the kids are still the same. Yesterday a child threw something at another child while I was leading my kids in. It hit me on my lip! The kids were cheering me on to let him have it back! Margo, you know that I wanted to (let the child have it!) I am putting it nicely but I locked my classroom door and walked to the office with a whole flight of children cheering me on with "fight", fight", "fight"! I told the vice-principal what happened and walked back to class annoyed.

Girl, some days I wish it would rain so hard that school would be canceled. I can't complain though, despite everything that has happened in error for the year, God has proven Himself faithful to me and my son's father. Sometimes I feel so bad when we get into arguments because He has blessed me with a great man. I look at him as a great old novel. The more you read it, the more you get to understand and love it, even though the pages are tattered! I am missing you so much and I can't wait to see you guys. The house is still in ruin and we are still renovating. Kiss the baby and we will catch up!

Your Friend,

Liz

AILING HANDS

Fitzroy Oswald Emilio, her father, enjoyed taking long walks on Friday nights with her brother and herself to a forested field that was favored as the baseball park in San Nicholas, Aruba. He loved baseball and because he favored this sport, she loved it just the same! Her father was a thrill seeker and he lived life to the fullest. Regardless of how much adventure he sought, she admired him for the way that he respected her mother and honored his marital vows.

Her father had the handsomeness of an army boy and a streamlined body that sailed through the Caribbean seas on lazy days. When she was old enough to understand, she realized that Parkinson's was there to stay even though it was an unwelcomed visitor which riddled his able body with bedsores in his last days. She could still picture her father sitting in his recliner aged by use and frequent moisture, and she smiled! His daily routine included combing his woolen hair. This was done before he ate the hefty breakfast that her mama prepared. He also spent countless hours nursing thirsty seedlings. Sometimes he frequented book stores and he fed his hunger for knowledge by reading and purchasing books! She saw the fire that burned in her father's eyes slowly deteriorate after he and his coworkers got laid off. Parkinson's only seemed to take effect on his body after he stopped going to work.

There was not one day that either one of them had to purposely visit a library for information to complete a project. Every area of life was covered by a book or pamphlet that her dad piled high in his office that never seemed to be in order. Her father was the only one that was able to place his hands on a book if anyone needed it. He found order in all what seemed to be a mess and confusion in her mind. He was unique in every way from the way he slurped his tea, to the way he would slump in his chair and twitch uncontrollably. His body was at war with the enemy, for many hours on certain days. There was a skillful way his ailing hands held his comb. Her father touched many lives for his uprightness in the community by his stance on religion, his love for his wife and his children but more so for the way, his hands cradled them all in family photographs, just as how a hen cradles her chicks in her bosom when it is storming.

Can you imagine that even though his hands twitched often, they earned a living for their family and embraced her mother in times of weakness and endearment? Those ailing hands disciplined her brother when he seemingly was going astray, but those same hands lifted her over puddles in the street that was too huge for her tiny feet to cross. Those same hands held her hand while crossing busy streets!

PRIZED LAND

Grandpa spent numerous days, relaxing and taking in the sweet smell of Mountain coffee. He sat in his wooden chair aged by years of use and listened keenly to the melodious chant of birds on his coffee plantation.

He got really angry but there was nothing that he could do at this point. Those birds knew that he was tired of chasing them out of his trees. In the past, when he tried to chase them by aiming his shotgun in the air and giving them some warnings, they would only fly away and later come back, mocking him with their chirps as he slept on his porch.

He would even awaken to find them doing annoying bird dances on the mud window sills. Some were bold enough to leave droppings on his dining table on the porch. Although these creatures had the power to make a beautiful day on a Jamaican coffee farm go sour, he was happy to be alive!

Grandpa's body ached from years of breaking huge stones into gravel for the rich people's yards. This, along with the lack of help pained his back so he reached for the sore area and rubbed it. He then swatted a black and white mosquito that was biting him on his crusty foot.

Grandpa repositioned himself, passed gas, and began reminiscing. The sound of; "HILTON, I am coming to give you your injection", jolted him back to reality as he rubbed the sore part of his shoulder. Though Aunt Beryl was not even a trained nurse she willingly pierced his skin with this weapon.

He disliked the needles and the strict diet that the doctor placed him on. A pleasant smile filled Grandpa's face as thoughts of the Jamaican white rum teased his mental state. He could feel its tingle in his throat and he could not wait for Aunt Beryl to leave so that he could send Uncle Desmond to buy him a bottle! Every time he tried to drink his rum and coke it would only cause his hands to become stiff and he would sit on the porch and moan!

Grandpa saw the gleam in Beryl's bloodshot eyes. This made him frightened and he pulled away and shouted: "Beryl I hope that you have wiped off that needle with alcohol," Do you know what you are about to do"? Beryl ignored his usual mutterings, packed up the needles and walked into the family room.

His urge to urinate often came from him having sugar. He reached for his wooden walking stick, muscled himself over to grandma's room, peeped in on her, and then practically hopped over to the middle bedroom. The burning in his groin caused him to walk faster to the bathroom and not worry to linger in Uncle Desmond's bedroom.

One of the nails that was sticking up from the floorboards conveniently hitched itself in Grandpa's shoe heel and caused him to stumble headfirst. Urine and everything came spilling out of Grandpa's body, as he fell. That was the first time in his life he felt helpless! All he wanted was to close his eyes and let his soul be at peace, but he realized that Grandma needed him and that was enough for him to hold on.

He tried to open his mouth to call for help, but he did not realize that the messages from his brain were not reaching his mouth or so he thought. He tried several times and he lay there in hope that one of his children would help him!

Several hours passed by and Aunt Beryl wondered why Grandpa was not at his usual post on the verandah. Beryl called; "Papa"! "Papa"! Grandma answered that he was probably outside. Aunt Beryl was on her way to the back of the house and realized that Grandpa was slumped down on the wooden floor.

Beryl ran to his side, threw his arms over her shoulders, and helped him into his bed. Beryl realized that he could not walk on his own. She also noticed that he was not speaking. The weekend went by and Beryl had to travel back to Kingston, her newfound home.

Beryl felt a bit concerned about what her sisters or brothers would think. How would they view her, if she left Grandpa bedridden without leaving someone to take care of him? She then entered the taxi that drove into the plantation. Her worries about Grandpa were also forgotten after all she was not the only child. Aunt Beryl's mind and interests were elsewhere.

Grandpa Hilton was thankful that he was at rest in his hospital bed. Aunt Minerva who was a grade school teacher rushed him to the hospital days after, in her grey Toyota car. She rushed to Grandpa Hilton after having received the call from her brother Desmond about her father. Grandpa Hilton was bedridden and not able to speak. Grandpa now knew the motives of his last daughter Beryl.

It was all too clear to him now that if he was left in his state at home he would have died and his prized land would have been all hers. Aunt Beryl constantly grumbled and complained about others being his favorites and she secretly hated that! Grandpa missed the years of reaping harvest on his estate. He smiled at remembering the secret rendezvous with Grandma and the many years of celebrations of life. He then nodded his head at the loss of loved ones who were called home.

He felt relieved after eating some warm soup. Aunt Minerva was informed about the minor stroke that Grandpa Hilton had after he was finished with the varied tests at the hospital. It was the reason why he was briefly unable to speak. Four-thirty finally came and Aunt Minerva rushed to the hospital to help Grandpa into the car.

They drove for hours and as the eve marched in they arrived at the plantation. Everyone was there to welcome Grandpa back home except Beryl!

FORBIDDEN LOVE

Yvette loved the way that Dean would look at her. It only took one glance from his dreamy island eyes for Yvette to feel the waves of emotion flooding her soul. It was exactly one year after Dean met Yvette on a trip to Jamaica and their romance budded quickly. They spent many long hours in each other's arms at night. Dean was extremely jealous and overprotective, this bothered her a lot. She was never allowed to go to the store or the mall by herself anymore.

Everywhere that Yvette now went Dean went as well! She wanted her freedom back, but she did not want to lose him. He paid all of her bills and made sure that whatever needed fixing around the house would get done. It was just that one day Yvette decided to smile at another man while they were on a date. Dean's response to Yvette was a real surprise! He held her arm and squeezed it hard she could not believe that Shawn would act harshly because of an innocent smile towards another male.

Everything started to go sour, even her feelings towards him. He started to beat her with a passion and she became angry. Yvette would make sure that his dinner was cooked before he came home. She also paid keen attention to cleaning the house. Everything would be in place. She thought that doing these things would change him. It seemed that the more she tried to be on his good side that the beatings became frequent. Yvette realized that whatever she tried to do to make him happy, still did not change his attitude. This caused her to get down on her knees to pray. She always saw her mother praying and in the past prayer worked for her. Yvette prayed day in and day out and patiently waited!

The days went by and the beatings became frequent. To her, it became routine for her male friend to let all of his tension out on her through her daily doses of beatings. "Boy was life strange", her friends received a release of tension from their male counterparts in one aspect and she received it in another! The worst possible kind that man could ever dream of, but Yvette stayed faithful and she prayed, and she took her beatings and she prayed! One day as Yvette was in the sturdy mud house doing her honorary duties, she happened to look out through the windows. She saw a couple of butterflies happily flying in and around the Nooney Tree. She smiled as she focused on this site, which she never really cared to pay much attention to. This brought her great joy! Yvette continued to look on. She found it strange that there were other rose bushes, plants and fruit trees in the orange dirt garden, but not one of those butterflies paid any of those plants attention! She focused all of her attention on these little insects. This caused her not to hear or see Dean's car pulling into the driveway. He opened the door, walked in and called out her name. She still did not acknowledge his presence! He felt that he was always respected and treated as such, in the community. It annoyed him that Yvette chose to ignore him or so he thought. He walked up behind her and laced her skin with multiple lashes from his leather belt. Yvette cried as the lashes cut into her skin. He went into the bedroom and started undressing, as he was finished with his sacred ritual.

He needed to wash off the dirt and grime and the usual annoyance of having to deal with his thoughts about Yvette's attitude.

SHATTERED

The turquoise waters looked quite welcoming as Diamond stood on the cliff, looking down. A hurt feeling overpowered Diamond as she stood there looking down over the waters. I guess she stood there just trying to gain composure. She needed all the strength that she had left in her body to keep herself from crying—not only crying but ending up in a frenzied state. Diamond was in a temporary state of shock, and it showed on her face. Diamond hugged herself tightly as the cool Caribbean breeze blew against her dark skin.

There were all kinds of thoughts that ran through her mind—thoughts as to why mankind was so cruel to her and why the world was always dishing out the worst. Well, Diamond could not seem to find the answers to these questions that plagued her mind. All she knew was that she was tired of life's troubles—tired of being used, first of all, and then, in the end, being abused.

Day in, day out, as a little island girl attending primary school, Diamond had to take the constant teasing and humiliation from the children at school. Why? I guess society did not acknowledge the essence of uniqueness and being different. So Diamond never seemed to feel comfortable around anyone; she just preferred to be left alone. Then she did not have to worry about being in anyone's way. That still did not stop the other school children from teasing her. It only seemed to make it worse for her. When she was out of earshot of those who teased her, they still managed to get to her in ways that could only be dreamed of. Some would shoot spitballs made out of chewed-up straws at her when she was out of earshot of those who teased her.

Diamond caught her breath as her eyes misted as she began to remember all the horrid things that happened to her while she was growing up. All of those who were not shooting the spitballs at her were either pulling her hair or throwing rocks at her after school. Diamond felt all her painful past sweep over her like a river filled with raging demons.

For years Diamond taught herself to live in seclusion and secrecy. She felt as if she could not trust anyone, not even her parents of West Indian descent. What Diamond found funny was that no matter how many counselors or psychologists she was referred to, no one could reach into her mind and understand what was going on in her brain. No Myers Briggs or any other personality test from the highest institute could assess her. No doctor could prescribe any suitable medication for her ailments, because no proper assessments of her condition could have been made. She was who she was, and she would remain the same complex individual. — She was all alone in a world by herself and left to fend for herself and her family.

Whatever the world dished out to her she took, and she tried to cope with it the best way she knew how.

Tears started to stream down Diamond's face as she remembered an incident that happened to her when she was eleven years old. It was the Christmas season and Diamond enjoyed the usual festivities that filled the air when she was on the islands. Diamond's nostrils took in the healthy smell of Christmas ham and turkey baking in the far distance from her house. Her favorites, though, were the smell of sweet potato pie, coconut tart, and cake.

One evening Diamond decided to take a stroll just to get her mind off of her predicament of being rather big and uncomfortable. Diamond decided to take a walk through her neighborhood to visit a neighbor. Diamond noticed a couple of street boys from around the way carelessly fooling around. A couple of these neighborhood boys were playing street basketball, and others were playing hooky with any young school girl that happened to pass close to their traps. Diamond paid these boys no attention and continued on her journey.

It was a beautiful afternoon to take a stroll, and she enjoyed it so much that on her way back to her house she took her time to enjoy the busy scene of the hustle and bustle of last-minute

Christmas preparations. While she was passing the same spot where the neighborhood boys were seen hanging out a few moments before, she found it strange that there was no one in sight besides a tattered-looking boy who was in his late twenties. Diamond paid this chap no mind and continued to walk despite his cheap whistles and nasty comments that were thrown at her.

As Diamond proceeded to walk on faster, she noticed that the boy's footsteps sped up behind her. His footsteps sped up, and because of fear, Diamond panicked and turned around and expected him to come to a halt. Despite her wishes for peace and calm, that devious imp gripped Diamond, held on to her, and placed her neck into a vicious headlock. Diamond tried with all her might to lose herself from his clammy hands that gripped her body at that point.

She tried to run, but every effort seemed useless. Diamond closed her eyes to block out what was happening to her. Diamond opened her mouth to issue a bloodcurdling scream, but guess what? Every time Diamond opened her mouth, no sounds came out! Did fright cause Diamond to lose her voice and also become frozen in place with fright? Maybe if Diamond closed her eyes and opened them again, she would realize that this was just a dream and any minute she would awaken from that dream.

Diamond tried that, but when she quickly reopened her eyes, the buttons on her blouse were carelessly dragged open. Her blue lace brassiere was exposed to that imp who still kept his vicious grip around her neck. Seeing Diamond's pear-shaped breasts caused an instant growth in this pervert's pants, and the sight of that made

Diamond's stomach queasy! One of the boy's hands was thrown around Diamond's neck, which kept her firmly in place, and the other was groping her breast. Diamond hated the feel of his hands caressing her body without her consent.

She was livid. Diamond got so angry that she started to see red circles bouncing around in front of her eyes. Who was he to violate her right to privacy and take away all her dignity in a matter of seconds? The seconds seemed like hours to Diamond. Diamond twisted her head into a position from which she had access to this boy's arm, and she took a generous bite out of his arm. The diamond bit that boy's arm until her frail teeth started to ache and until her taste buds got the salty taste of this beast's blood. Diamond was afraid that her teeth would lock into his arm and would not be freed, but her biting him saved her precious life!

Diamond was freed, with that quick action and she hurriedly fixed the buttons on her blouse back into place as she ran home. She was out of breath as she ran into her parents' home and her mother questioned her as to why she was out of breath. Diamond could only reply that a boy down the road had felt her up. Diamond did not expect her mother to respond in the way that she did to that horrid piece of information.

No one would have ever imagined that her mother would have laughed and then asked, "Who did what?" Diamond felt so hurt and embarrassed because the only person she was sure she could turn to in a time of need had laughed at her. Diamond heard in school that shock usually caused people to react differently. Her mother's reaction shocked her, and it caused her to realize that she could never again in her life reveal to her mother any hurtful incident that happened to her.

Bullets of salty water pierced Diamond's face. She did not realize that she was lying directly over the ocean's mouth, burying her sorrows over a watery grave. Trying to forget her past was difficult. It seemed rather impossible!

On numerous nights, Diamond lay awake on her moth-eaten mattress, haunted and scarred by her past. This event brought back memories of that lonely winter night in a foreign country, and Diamond decided to journey back home on a bus. The bus cried out when the driver turned out from the station as if to say "Why did you pack me over the limit?"

Every seat and passageway was filled! Inch by inch, passengers got off at their exits, and it seemed that she was left alone on the long stretch home. It was then 11:45 p.m. Diamond looked up into the rear-view mirror just in time to notice that she was not alone.

There was a strange character half asleep on the bus. Diamond decided that the strange character posed no instant threat. She then settled in her seat and looked outside. She felt an eerie, threatening presence as she awoke to find the strange character grinning at her face as he squeezed himself more into her seat. Diamond felt fear choking her.

Why this man was seemingly a crackhead imposing on her confined space! Diamond's teary eyes sought help from the bus driver in the rear-view mirror as the man proceeded to try to get closer. He did so in ways that were unimaginable to Diamond at this point. Diamond felt the hatred rising, as she remembered all the times that people had taken advantage of her. Most of the time, she did nothing about the occurrences. Diamond knew that if this beast did not leave her alone, she would start to vent all of her anger on this drugged-up mute and give him his just dessert!

She could not believe that the bus driver saw what was going on and did nothing about it! It was as if the bus driver was enjoying the performance started by this crude character! Diamond was too happy to see her exit and gladly pushed herself past this addict and exited the bus. Diamond got off the bus and ran all the way home.

Diamond ran as fast as her feet could carry her weight! Not one minute did she look back to see if that man had also gotten off the bus and followed her. Diamond was happy that her hands did not fumble when she put the keys in the lock and the door opened! She quickly locked the door and ran to her room!

In the solace of her room, Diamond stripped off her clothes and leaned herself against the door, and cried as if one of her loved ones had died. Somehow Diamond found herself in the shower and she let the warm water erase the remnants of that rogue that clung to her. She scrubbed her skin so hard that she was sore and red.

She now crossed her long brown legs as she tried to chase away one of the island's hungry beasts, a black and white mosquito! Despite that, Diamond enjoyed being on the islands. She loved the spicy food and she admired what the spicy food did to the native men. In her mind, she also felt that the food helped to create such feisty women! It was really difficult living around so many women, especially single mothers. Or so she thought!

Despite the many hardships that these mothers encountered, they still found a way to instill the will for success into their offspring. What made Diamond happy at this point was that she finally found a place where she would have the chance to integrate into the culture. The Caribbean would be called her home and she would be at ease here!

TORN

It was five o'clock in the morning and neighbors were already stirring, trying to do last-minute preparations before the hurricane hit. Black, heavy storm clouds masqueraded around the towering hills as the meteorologist squealed his repetitious chant: "Folks be prepared: the hurricane is coming!"

The minutes slowly ticked on and the hours crawled by! But why was this storm—or should I say hurricane—interrupting our scheduled life? Teachers had classes to teach and students had classes to attend. Businessmen had deals to make and merchandise to sell.

Let's not forget the streetwalkers who paraded their bodies for a puny commission. It was hard to understand why the air buzzed with an eerie uncertainty that this storm would meet and leave behind. Looking back up at the hills that surrounded my parents' prefabricated fortress, there was no telling now what this monstrous beast had in store for our island. Deep down in my heart, I was praying for this storm to hit so that school would be canceled.

Any person would wish the same if they were in my shoes, especially facing Fourth-form preparation for competitive Caribbean Examinations Council examinations. Now, my intentions seemed selfish and I asked God to forgive me for my horrid sins. I prayed for an intervention, and oh my goodness, would this be the world's end? So many questions ran through my mind and the only thing that seemed to calm me was that this storm would hopefully be over in a couple of hours. Well, that's what I thought!

Taking my position at the dining room window, I peeped through the board that tried to serve as a barrier to the raging winds that tormented the community. I noticed certain houses ceased to stand. The hurricane was not scheduled for arrival until a few hours later. Strange enough, felt rooftops were sailing through the air!

Some roofs landed in our yard. The most painful experience was when they started to land on our house with horrible booms and crashes! At this point, I was only grateful that Mama had already started dinner and it was near completion. When I peeped outside again, I saw that most of the houses were flat on the ground. I wondered in my heart how many people had escaped to safety and how many ill fates befell?

While all these questions ran through my mind, I wondered why I smelled gas? Maybe it was just my mind playing tricks on me. After all, the subconscious has been considered a powerful being. I did not mention anything to my family at that point, because I wanted to be sure of my discovery. My parents then realized that there was gas seeping into the house from the gas tanks.

My parents started to panic; at least Mama did as she pulled at her weave and called out to God simultaneously. My father decided to make a quick dash outside to rectify the problem. My mother gave him a towel to wrap his head in and told him to be careful. There were rusty pieces of aluminum roof sheets flying through the air and I wondered if my father would be safe.

I looked around at my brother to see how he was feeling, but his face told me that he was clueless. He showed no emotion on his face. I realized that my mother was in a state of confusion because she was pacing the living room. I wondered if she thought that her pacing would help the problem at hand.

Just then my father ran in. We were shocked to hear that our gas tanks had been knocked down by falling debris from a neighbor's house. The electricity was turned off at dawn, which forced us to light numerous candles and lamps in the living room, which was adjacent to our kitchen. It was only God's mercy that saved us from not being blown up in our house.

My father consoled us that the gas tanks were turned off, and we prayed for the best at that point. I could not hold myself together, any more so I let my tears go. Our house seemed to stand as an airport for all the landing debris from other people's houses. Huge iron beams punched the roof to get a better view of our living room while I was standing in the living room.

The beams welcomed themselves to our house whichever way they deemed fit, but I was not having it! I rebuked the storm and those selfish beams in God's name. I then wondered how many people were in the same predicament. Were they also calling on the name of God for help?

We decided to move to another room for shelter after the iron beams visited our house through the wrong entrance, our roof. It made me mad inside to see that our house was slowly being torn apart by the tides of the storm. There was now an inch of water on the floor and I was tired of this reckless situation. Every minute we were trying to run from room to room as if we were trying to hide from death.

At this point, my expressions displayed an unaffected attitude. If I was to be killed in this storm, then so was it, even though I wanted to live to experience college. I looked up through the holes in the roof and I could see the raging storm as I dragged my feet through the water. This only made my tears flow faster!

I finally slumped down into a corner of the family washroom and tried to keep myself from losing my mind. I hugged myself tightly as if that was some measure of reassurance. All I discovered was that I was shaking uncontrollably. Unrecognized grunts ripped from my body in response to the devil's symphony. It was playing amid the storm. It seemed useless at the moment, but I tried to control my tears.

One would think that I would get comfort from knowing that the skies were pitch black. I still did not—all because I knew that it was only midday. I tried to make up my mind to make the best of the storm. I laid back against one of the three concrete partitions of our washroom. Here, my family chanted songs of mercy as loudly as they could over the wiles of the storm. Maybe if someone had heard us, they would have saved us from our house; at least that's what I had hoped.

I felt that I was not going to see the light of another day. So many conflicting thoughts were running through my mind. My parents seemed to have begun to lose hope too when our little washroom started to take a nasty beating from flailing debris. I was tired of feeling afraid, and that made my stomach feel queasy.

I ignored the sensation of losing my dinner and wished for the storm to be over. It was rather amazing that we could still pick up the frequency from a neighbouring island's radio station. The newscaster announced that Sint Maarten still had a few more hours before the category-four hurricane would hit!

I started to hate everything around me. I hated my parents for having me and my brother for being so loving to everyone around him. I even despised my noisy dog, Tiger", wondering if he was riding out the storm as a true soldier. Sad to say, I even started to wonder where God was in all of this?

Had He forsaken us when we needed Him? Or was this His lesson for us? I tried to seek comfort in the idea that we would be safe throughout the storm, by us riding it out in the washroom. Little did I know!

Just then, a heavy iron beam hurled itself through one of the washroom's windows, aimed straight at Mama's head. A bloodcurdling scream ripped from my hoarse throat. Seconds ago, my mother had been standing up in the washroom, trying to get herself settled into a comfortable place on the floor. Luckily, she stooped down to look at something that was crazily crawling on the floor and colliding into the wall with other things in the room.

Could it be that this horrid insect was also confused? I made up my mind that I was getting tired—tired of trying to fight this storm. My father suggested that we should move to the second bathroom adjacent to my room since it was a complete four-walled structure. This bathroom was the smaller of the two, but it was also one block higher than the other rooms in the house.

After all, what other place could be safe in the house if the concrete addition was frail and unsafe? Earlier on in the afternoon, all bedroom doors had been locked from the outside. I stared at my parents strangely, wondering why they were wasting their time. This Hurricane Luis was very determined, and he seemed to stop at nothing just to have his last say. I remembered the fear that locked me into an upward position outside of my parent's bedroom door as I stared at the wall.

The wall was split in two, nakedly exposing the fiberglass that seemed to be haphazardly stuffed into the walls. Drops of salty water gnawed my face, as I stood there staring in disbelief. There were continuous efforts of mass destruction made by this unruly hurricane. He had a purpose and was not going to leave until he fulfilled it!

One thing I knew for sure at this point: I needed to pull myself together. Every horrid boom or crash that echoed in my ears caused me to jump! I started to wonder when the debris that was tormenting the house would find itself in and hit either one of us? I did not exactly remember our passage from the washroom to the bathroom, but I remembered looking up into the living room's roof because the water was profusely pouring down into the house.

My family tried to fit any and everything that they could fit into hefty plastic bags, in the earlier part of the morning. Certain things such as books and knickknacks were packed in boxes and taken up off of the floor. The furniture and other electrical appliances were covered with plastic. I could imagine the frustration in my family's minds. What was not wet before was now swollen with water.

I sat in a tight corner of the shower with my brother and Mama huddled right next to me with pillows and blankets. My father sat beside the door facing the face basin. I guess that this was it for the night. We were going to be true conquerors and persevere the ill tide, even though the fierce wind raged outside the bathroom's door. It seemed angry due to it not finding a way into our premises.

The wooden door seemed to offer me a false sense of security. I wondered how much longer it would have been before the raging storm would have forced itself into the bathroom and tear it apart? Other questions plagued my mind as to what state our house was in? Was it now just a skeleton in ruin?

The walls tried to give in to the pressure. The strain that they faced caused the walls to squeal out with pain. The deafening crashes, the atomic booms, the deathly thumps and wails caused my head to ache! My pulsing headache caused my eyes to hurt, and I was weary from the taste of blood that kept resurfacing in my throat.

Through all of this, my soul ached and my puffy, bloodshot eyes tried to see. I was so preoccupied in my world that I simply did not hear my parents discussing that we were going to make another dash to a spare concrete room that was attached to the front of our house. I did not see the relevance of this decision. Were we to be aimlessly running from room to room, and then how long would it be before we would be maimed or even killed?

Despite my thoughts, I had to follow suit—follow my parents' orders. Each of us proceeded to quickly wrap ourselves in blankets, making sure that our heads were carefully covered. In my father's frail state, he opened the door and each of us grabbed stuff that we dragged from room to room. My father and my brother grabbed the smoky lamps.

I was really happy that my parents were a bit old-fashioned and believed in always having kerosene lamps at their disposal. Can you imagine wading through a waterfall with a lit candle? I felt sorry for anyone who was left to fight the darkness with candles that would be difficult or even impossible to rekindle if the wicks were wet.

Stepping down into the hallway was like stepping into a swimming pool.

It made no sense to me that we were leaving a dry bathroom to wade through inches of water that would lead to immeasurable uncertainties past the dining room and the adjoining kitchen. The only comfort that I found at this point was the sight of our now frail house still holding on for its dear life. Trudging through inches of water, we finally got to the front room. Stepping down into this room, we realized that this room served as a reservoir for the falling water that poured down on our heads from the gashes in the roof's stomach.

I was so upset that I could taste the anger that was causing my blood to bubble through my veins. My anger now caused me to see the dark images in crimson red. Why did we leave the comfort of a dry bathroom to end up in this? All of the rooms seemed to offer false security?

Was this beast of a hurricane using all of his resources to make us feel that way? Well, at least this room was bigger and we had more room to move around and stretch our cramped feet. My father said to the family that it would be wise for us to lie down on the floor. I tried to make sense out of nonsense, but I followed instructions and took my dry pillow and laid it in the water. The decision was then made to go to sleep in a watery grave.

If the fallen debris did not kill me, then I would surely catch my death from pneumonia. I wished and prayed that God would just end this hurricane, as I closed my eyes tightly. I sobbed softly under the thunderous noises of the storm, praying that my wish would come true. My body trembled as I continuously sobbed and tried to ward off the sick feeling of shivering.

I felt lonely lying in this dirty water, amid the confusion and disarray. Maybe it was due to both of my parents and my brother being quiet. Were they experiencing the same emotions as I was? Or did they think it wise to just remain quiet at the last moments of their lives?

Little did I know that we were not going to ride out the remaining part of the hurricane here. That was what I faintly understood as I woke from my watery grave. My father suggested that if we were to live we should make a run for our neighbor's home and find safety there. How silly we were to venture out of our slightly flooded home to risk losing our lives?

I continued to sit quietly in the water and hoped that my family would change their mind about venturing out into the darkness and wiles of the storm. I realized that the storm had calmed down as I sat there. There were no more loud noises echoing through the room, only the pitter-patter of raindrops as they fell on our heads. Then and there my father ran to the dining-room door and we foolishly followed suit. I did not question anyone's actions.

All I knew was that I did not want to be left alone in this crumbling prefabricated pad. We saw lanterns and life over at our neighbor's house, as we stood at the door. We welcomed the signs of life for all around us was squalor. There were hardly any homes left standing, only useless toilets. There was no running water, and there was hardly any food.

This was indeed a crisis! How would families react to seeing that they had lost everything upon return? Would this storm damage our economy and would we go back to the good old days? Would we have to be like the people who read by smoky, old lamps? All these questions ran through my mind, but would I find answers for each one?

There was no time, though, to entertain my thoughts. We wrapped our heads in towels and we bid each other a safe passage to our neighbor's home. That was where we rode out the storm. We wished for the raging storm to leave our island and not overstay his welcome. It felt as if two days had passed by as we walked across our road—or what was left of our road—back to our humble abode. Everything seemed to be okay with our home, except for a couple of wires and beams that were helplessly hanging from our verandah's roof.

Our dog even looked happy, for the simple fact that he was free to roam the streets without any restraint and without having anyone to harass him with orders. He was in charge now and he was happy. Even signs of his wooden shed were nowhere in sight. My father proceeded to call his name: "Brutus, Brutus." Can you imagine that?

That dog simply ignored his master's call and proceeded to defecate on the neighbor's front lawn. The lawn was now all messed up with debris from other houses. My father called his name again, and to my surprise, he snarled and bared his teeth at my father, as if to say "You better not try to come and catch me and tie me up, or else I will bite you!" I found it funny that our dog behaved that way!

We saw that our dog was tired of being tied up and was not about to be following rules anymore, so we left him alone. We wondered what ill circumstances our eyes would behold beyond the walls. That was before we entered the house. Could we have managed whatever it was that was behind the walls? Would we have been able to handle the after-effects of what society and that wall had fooled us into thinking, of providing security and shelter?

We were really surprised as we entered the house and saw that the house was still standing.

The kitchen, living room, bathrooms, and bedrooms were all still there. Oh my goodness! I was just about to jump for joy that our whole house was still standing. That changed when I opened the door to my bedroom. My wall had burst open and a bit of its stomach was showing.

A feeling of nausea overtook me. I only hoped at that moment that the other two bedrooms in the house were still standing. I was irate at this point. How could higher heads okay such permits to build the monstrous death traps for islanders to live in?

I walked slowly to my parent's room, and I barely opened the door, when my nose was welcomed by itchy wads of fiberglass. Now I tried to see why the pieces of fiberglass were floating around and not really in their assigned places, which were supposed to have been between the sheetrock. I did not want to blame them, because they were like Bruno, our stubborn dog. He looked like he was having the time of his life, being free, roaming the streets and getting into uncalled-for mischief that he was only able to dream of before when he was on a leash.

Now he was able to live life to the fullest. Hmm, he must have been somewhere watering unwanted seeds. Well, as the air cleared and I looked around, I saw that the wall was completely torn down the center as if God was upset and took a piece of paper and ripped it in two. Was God really mad at mankind?

Why had this happened? Or was it an act of nature that had just occurred, or was it God's way of speaking and telling us to get our souls right with him? I suppose that it was God that spoke. Would these islanders heed his call?

Would they make things right with themselves and their neighbors? Would they teach their young ones the value of having respect? Would this change the chaotic existence? Well, only time would tell!

I wondered how the wall would have been repaired, as I switched my focus to it? The person deemed with taking on the task of repairs would have to be called ingenious for taking up such a craft and having the know-how to execute the art! I then moved to another room to check the damage. To my surprise, all the walls in the third room were okay: no tears or any broken structures. Well, the only broken structure that was present was the house and it needed to be rebuilt, and fast too!

FAMILY SECRETS

Mosquitoes busied themselves on Colleen's meager legs, as she tried to peep at Uncle Clarence. Colleen was perched on an uprooted Ackee tree that was flung aside from the island's last storm. It was extremely hot and she was sure that Clarence was in the mood for some of his ridiculous hide-and-go-seek games.

Colleen had just cleared up the breakfast dishes and she promised herself to take a half an hour's break. She knew that hardly anyone knew about her secret spot in the clearing behind the pigs' pen. Clarence was the only one and he was recently compensating her for her sexual favors that he was too busy to get from one of the street girls.

Clarence continued to pace the parched yard. He heard his father bellowing: "Clarence,

Clarence, come here". He decided to give up the search for Colleen and go inside. Colleen gave a sigh of relief but she knew that he would be back. It was Saturday and she also knew that his sister Vanny would be coming by soon from Mandeville.

Clarence and the rest of the family thought that Vanny made that sacrificial visit each month's end to bring groceries for the household. But Colleen knew differently. Even Vanny's husband Melford was fooled.

Vanny would wear the tightest, sophomore dresses that she could find. Colleen found it impossible that she was a pastor's wife. She even wondered how she could catch the Holy Spirit in some of the outfits that she paraded her figure-eight-shaped body in.

One Saturday morning Colleen gave an excuse about not being able to make breakfast for the household. She hardly got any free days so she decided to spend the day in Santa Cruz. She was on her way to the taxi stand when she saw Vanny leaning in to kiss Mr. Chris, the community's wealthiest restaurant owner.

Certain things started to make sense to her. She wondered why Vanny took so long to drive into Grandpa's yard. She also wondered why Vanny entered the yard with a bounce in her step with her face all lit up. Everyone knew that her husband Melford was also wealthy but she was not allowed to spend his money as she pleased!

She hurried past the restaurant and she could have felt sorry for Melford but he was mean and miserable. He was a preacher who had dirty secrets of his own. Colleen realized that his wife's niece's daughter was the mirror image of his daughter.

She noticed this during the last family reunion when all the cousins were gathered in the family's room.

That same niece; Merline, snuck up into the hills with Melford to frolic. Colleen enjoyed hiding in the clearings on these days. That would be when she would discover all the shocking family secrets.

Colleen noticed Miss May as she made her way to the taxi stand. She was the lady that frequently visited Grandpa with colorful sugar cakes. When she visited, she would rub Grandpa's hands and laugh at all of his jokes. Trouble came when Miss May's hands went too far one day and started to rub Grandpa's shoulders. Lira; grandpa's wife chased her off the porch with a mouth full of colorful words that did not include anything from Sunday's sermon!

Lira was angry and she was not going to let a careless old lady come in and steal grandpa right from under her nose. His body was usually pained up but to her, he was great company! Colleen hailed Miss May and proceeded to get into a taxi. Her mind was so full of what crazy things were going on in the Reed family. She tried to settle it though by looking at the people she saw as they zoomed past in the old white Toyota.

Colleen noticed that the streets were lined with many vendors as the car pulled into Santa Cruz. They were chanting the names of their products to passersby. Some were even bold enough to hold onto busy people who were in a rush to get back to work or get from one point to another. This was what Colleen enjoyed, the sweet smell of market produce, brewing confusion, and festive island life!

Colleen's thoughts began to refocus on Miss May and her unhidden feelings for Grandpa. Her mind even strayed to her countless moments that were stolen away in the mountains with Clarence. Most of the time she pretended to enjoy them but since he was unwilling to commit to her, she decided to make him pay for her services!

She would drop in by the clinic and refill her prescription. She waited for her prescription while Dr. White coaxed one of his patients to come in for their results. The patient seemed hesitant over the phone. Dr. White was finished with his phone conversation when he greeted Colleen with his coffee-stained teeth. She bade him hurry because she wanted to reach back to Malvern before "*Young and The Restless*" came on.

Colleen was about to leave when he told her that her blood work results came back and that they were positive! She was confused and asked what he had meant by that? He told her that she should seek counseling at church or from an organization. Colleen's mind began to replay scenes from her life as if it were the movies as Dr. White continued to speak! All she could think about was how in the world she would be able to deal with having an incurable disease in the future?

Could this be the reason why Clarence tried to hide these oozing sores with his father's ointment and gauze pads? Was this the reason why he was only skin and bone? Oh goodness! Was this the reason why Clarence constantly complained about the chills when it was hot outside? Truly this was the ultimate family secret; she contracted HIV from Clarence!

STRUCK

The Malvern Hills seemed to lay lazily behind the grey clouds that were forecasted earlier in the morning to bring torrents of rain. The place seemed cold and dark yet for some strange reason quite still. This was a sure sign to Mama that bad weather was on the way. It was market day and unless there were darts of fire falling from heaven, she was sure to be on an area taxi to the market.

She bundled her head with her usual worn rags that reeked of Canadian Healing oil. She made sure that her head was prepared for the weight that her basket usually tried to force on her. She banded her spiny waist with her broad belt. She kissed Mass Jones on her way to the outside kitchen.

Mama nearly stumbled on the pickax that was filled with the orange dirt that lined their acred farm that yielded so much produce and wealth. Although she felt the years of strain take their toll on her frail body; she bent down and searched for the best fruits. The crop-ready tourist would pay top dollar for them.

Mama was pleased with her choice and she stepped back to look at her sweet-smelling pick of fruits. Even the fruit flies seemed drunk from the smell and they hovered over her pick. Mama stared at her produce and she wished that the basket would somehow lift itself unto her head without any effort on her part but she knew better.

"Baadam bang, badda blam" was the tune that the thunder played. She hoisted the basket unto her head and walked out the door. Mama felt her chest tighten as it searched for means to store the oxygen that her puny body so needed.

She was finally at the top of her stony lane and she was happy to see Steve. He was the most reliable taxi man and he understood the language that the poor people's pocket spoke. Mama was just about to wave Steve down when she saw the first sign of lightning as it rolled past her feet.

She refused to look back to see the resting place of the fiery serpent. Steve quickly pulled to the side and bid Mama to get in. He wanted to race the bad weather and get back home and be in the comfort of his wife's warm embrace.

Mama wondered if she had made a wise choice by still attempting to go to the market. Steve's taxi carried the usual perfume of cigarettes' envied cousin. The seats in Steve's taxi seemed to proudly wear the perfume just like the way that new clothes wore their pungent odour in pride.

There was hardly any traffic on the road and Mama then realized that for once, her fellowmen took the weatherman's warnings seriously. The taxi made an abrupt stop and Mama's body was nearly flung through the windshield. Mama forgot to sit in front of the taxi. That was the only place that Mama was guaranteed a seat belt.

The back seats were worn and had no care for holding people in place. Steve pulled up into the marketplace in Santa Cruz. He ordered Mama to get out quickly. Steve hurriedly popped the car trunk and Mama hoisted the heavy basket unto her head. She was so taken up with walking to her stall that she missed the ball of lightning that carelessly rolled past her feet. She tried to make it across the road with the heavy bundle on her head. She was soon to put it down when the thunder rolled and the lightning flashed!

That was the last thing that Mama remembered. She did not know how long she was passed out, or for how much was said to her. After a while, she did hear the voices of a cluster of noisy people chanting over her,

"Moomy, moomy, wake up, speak to us"!
"Open yuh eyes dem mi dear! Blink yuh eye dem if yuh can hear wi". "Lawd misses, do git up. Lawd Jesus, dissa one dead now"!

Her head hurt but she saw the happy tears of concerned people as she opened her eyes. She also saw a basket of fresh produce strewn along the ground. She tried to stabilize her feet and brush herself off. She saw that her clothes were all torn, soaked and burnt. It seemed to her that she was struck! Yes, struck by lightning!

She looked around and noticed that there were a handful of vendors left. Others were busy packing up their baskets and boxes to head home. There were still a couple of people who lingered close by to see if she would remain conscious or return to her earlier state. Her body felt as if she had taken a good dose of prickly pears. There was one problem though. She did not know where her home was and to who she was supposed to go home too.

She felt the pressure rising in her head. She decided to lean on one of the stalls nearby and wait for a Saviour. A car stopped close to the stall and a young man seemingly called out to her. *"Mama Trudy, you alright? Why yuh look so? Talk nuh, ma! Wha do yuh?* She looked on in a confused state. The young man got out of the taxi and walked towards her.

Mama Trudy stared at the man that rapidly approached her in bewilderment. He continued to talk but she just continued to look right through him as if she was fixated. He stopped short of her and waved his hand in front of her face.

Mama's mind was brought to a present state as she was millions of miles away a couple of minutes ago. She looked at the last vendor who got unto a laden truck of farm produce that drove off. All that was now left, was the truck that kicked up some dirt, the empty stalls, an overturned basket, a man, and herself. She was not her usual self so he tried to hold her hand. She did not move.

She saw his intentions and automatically her body braced itself against the force that tried to move her. The man looked a bit perplexed at her. Her brain refused to allow her to remember who she was. Yet her brain was still healthy enough to send messages to her neurons and command them to hold her limbs in place. This was his queue to lift her from her frozen position, step over a strewn basket of fruits and place her into his car.

The car passed a mob of people at a junction. They seemed to be encouraging two hefty women who were exchanging ugly words at each other. She looked on not knowing what sparked the argument. The man who was sitting beside her babbled on. He said: "Yuh no see seh dem a probably a fight ova dem baby fada"! She was in a moving car that seemed to travel on for a long while.

He continued to drive for a long spell. He passed some watermelon farms, tomatoes, and corn. The car rode up a hill and unto a road that was made from crushed stones. It seemed normal for her to be in a car that was being driven with no sense of direction. The car finally came to a stop outside of a quaint home on a large farm that had an array of crops. She was intrigued with the way the road that was laden with white crushed rocks blended in with orange dirt.

The man stared at her and she did not know that she was supposed to get out. He gunned the engine and then pulled the keys out of the ignition. He did not peep his horn, but he got out, flexed his legs, and dusted off his Clarks' shoes. He came around the side of the car and then proceeded to let her out of the car. She heard the sweet sounds of reggae from a tiny clock radio which tried its best to imitate a large stereo. She started to sing along with the next song.

"Every day I love her just a little bit more, a little bit more, just a little bit more, and she loves me the same"!

She made herself comfortable as the man called out a name several times. No one seemed to answer. The man walked towards the back of the home and she decided to follow. He continued to call out; "anybody home"? The radio seemed a bit congested, as some static interrupted the smooth flow of the music. There was some silence after the static.

Then the man heard a sound that represented a pig squealing. Her father used to let her watch him butcher farm animals when she was little. She knew that sound anywhere. The man walked past the door and the sounds continued. Maybe the farmer decided to butcher animals in the home. It was rare for farmers to do that inside of their homes.

It would be insane to mess up such a beautiful home with frilly lace curtains and shiny wooden floors. The noises started to turn to grunts and she started to feel pain. When she was younger she told herself that she would never raise animals because she hated to see them suffer.

The man knocked on that door and it swung open. He said, "*Mass Jones, Mama Trudy get lik by one lightning ball*" "*Me did try fi call out to Yuh, but di radio did a blast and yuh neva did a ansa di fone*"!

The butchering that she thought was taking place was only a man and a woman communing. She was relieved and she walked back out to where the radio played and sat down on the sofa.

The lady that was in the room where the squeals came from, was dressed and out of the house. She wanted to ask the lady if she had seen the lightning storm that had occurred earlier. Both men were now outside talking. The man whose car she drove in a while ago was shouting at the other.

She continued to enjoy the music and swatted a mosquito that hungrily clung to her leg. She got tired of sitting on the sofa and she decided to go outside and take a walk. The men did not realize that she had gotten up from her post. Some neighbours were outside looking at her. She stopped for a while and admired a green lizard that was perched high in a particular tree that had a strange scent. She continued to walk up the road and started to follow the scent of coffee.

That was her favorite thing to do when she was younger. When she was younger, she would take in the scent of the coffee trees whenever her father and she would drive into their lane on market day. She saw the same lady that was in the house earlier, as she stood under the coffee tree. Why was Ina running so fast through the plantation?

She started to run back to the house to look for Mass Jones.

She saw Steve when she entered the house. *"Steve a wey di brute di dey"? "In fact, im caan cum bak on yah"! "Mi did a figa dis a gwaan fi a lang time" "Di gyal used fi bring suga cake fi im all di wile"!* Steve said: *Mama Trudy yuh get back yuh memory"! "From di market yuh did seem like yuh nuh memba much"!*

That was when it struck her that she did not only get hit by lightning but also walked in on Mass Jones having an affair.

INTERVIEW WITH RICHARD

How interesting it would be to be a fly on the wall of an interview room. Some of us are experts at stretching the truth. When asked if we have knowledge of the computer, we grin our teeth and answer, yes, I know all about the computer. When in truth the only technological device that you know of is the expensive phone which you bought from your tax return. Only God knows that if it falls into the water or drops, you would be under so much pressure. If only people knew.

Sometimes the pressures we face in life force us to do things that are not in our nature but because of that survival switch being turned on in our heads we lie. In Richard's case for instance the

The interviewer asked: How old are you?

Richard: *30 sa!*

Interviewer: *Do you own a car?*

Richard: *Yes, sir me have one boasti car mi nah go be late fi di job man, trust me! Richard adjusts himself well in the chair and answers without blinking his eyes.*

Interviewer: *How do I know that you are trustworthy?*

Richard: *Mi did ave plenti a job. Mi is as trustworthy as dey come!*

Interviewer: *Are you computer literate? Can you use a computer?*

Richard: *yeah man see mi fone dey. (Richard pulls out his expensive phone and shows it). Mi can go pan di intanet, surf pan i and dungload!*

Interview: *Can you drive a stick shift vehicle?*

Richard: *Of co-arse! Where mi cum fram, mi a di safest taxi driva dey pan di road!*

The interviewer looked ova the one-page resume that Richard submitted just two weeks ago and seemed pleased by his answers. He shook Richard's hand and promised to call him the following week.

Richard kept his poise and breathed a great sigh of relief. Only God knew what stress he was under. His last meal was just a day ago and he was so dizzy from the lack of food and sleep. He lacked sleep from late nights of planning daylight robberies. If people only knew the reason he drove slowly was because he could not see well. This was not something that he would ever tell a soul. Furthermore, him being able to drive the stick shift delivery truck would have to be an all-night learning experience.

It was too much to remember and keep track of everything he told people. It was starting to get to him. He knew that he would be making a change and getting this job would mean the world to him. Even the stress of his link constantly calling him for his money which he needed for making his passport to say:

Richard Reed

St. Elizabeth

Jamaica

His 59-year-old body was tired of pretending to be 30. Steve, a long-time bredren of his, saw his plight and invited him to service in the park. Richard knew that his girlfriend: Karen's father died, she lamented over the fact, and hit him up for a large sum of money. She was supposed to come back on yesterday's flight and there was no sign of her. He waited at Caribbean Airlines' exit and there was no Karen! He even asked one of the people who got off the plane if they had seen a lady with a curly black and brown weave, yellow blouse, tight blue pants, gold sneakers and blue nails. The lady seemed confused. He asked some more people and he felt really stupid when a town lady laughed at him.

If you are exhausted by the hand that you have been dealt in life, with constant trials and no one trustworthy enough to talk to, unsure about what you will eat tomorrow, constant nervousness about someone finding out about your immigration status, living with a deadly disease, not clear about where your soul will go after leading a careless life?

There is great news! Like Richard, some have been lied to, beaten, cheated on, left behind and stolen from. But there is a friend that you can go and tell all your secrets to and he is forgiving enough to still love, take you as a husband or wife, trust you, and even prepares a place for you after you die.

His name is Jesus! All you have to do is know that you have sinned, confess and pray the sinner's prayer!

Like Adam and Eve, the temptation was great. The sin was sweet but the aftermath was painful. They were cast out from the garden due to their disobedience and their giving into the serpent. The sin followed their children and has caused humanity to be what it is. Sacrifices had to be made to clear the sin and make things right.

Today my dear friends it is easier! Christ sent his son to die on the cross and that was the sacrifice. So, when we sin it is easy to admit our sin to God and then ask him to be our Lord and personal Saviour, then rest assured that our afterlife will be with our Creator.

Do not leave here without understanding His plan for our lives. You have been served! I too have changed my lifestyle. Would you please change yours?

SECRET SHOPPER

The sun seemed to be hiding in the orange sky. The ants were also feeling its effect as they crazily ran. May hated the fact that it was raining and that she had to walk to work. Chance, her present lover and sixth's child's father, was late again in giving her money. The thought of having to walk from the rustic post office in Malvern to the busy town of Santa Cruz annoyed her. Deep down in her heart, she knew that it was her constant appetite for mating that landed her in that predicament.

The rain pelted down on her back, and she tried to keep her head down to hide her shame as the neighbours from the nearby tenement yard passed in their cars. She was the only one who had so many children and hardly any earthly possessions to show for her numerous courtships in the cane pieces and pastures.

May felt ashamed of her past actions. To her, it seemed as if men took her innocence. They promised the world, but as soon as she thought that she could have depended on them, their promises soon disappeared into thin air! Her first relationship with her first lover went well because she slept with Juniour, a married man. She throve off the excitement and was lavished with an extravagant lifestyle until his significant other found out and threatened to kill her in an acid attack!

Her second lover was Trevor, a man that she met on her newly acquired computer that she worked tireless hours to get. This whirlwind courtship with the St. Mary resident yielded child number two and an incurable STD. She craved his warm body and his warm and passionate kisses. Her relationship with this lover went sour after she trusted him with three hundred seventy-eight thousand Jamaican dollars to build the first floor of her country dwelling.

Joshy was the result of her third fling with John, an overseas businessman who frequently visited Jamaica to invest in the bauxite industry. When she found out that she was carrying his son, he ordered her to get rid of it and promised to kill her if she didn't follow suit. May thought that this was her way out of poverty for herself and her family.

John lavished May with large amounts of money and even furnished her one-bedroom apartment with a settee and a colored TV. May even kept John posted on her monthly visits to her doctor. That was when she noticed that his visits became less and less. On one of his last visits, he threw the money for the termination of pregnancy on the bed where she was lying.

May convinced John that she got rid of their child. She was still sure to have her baby Josh, even though he rarely came around. She gave Josh to one of her neighbours who was having problems with conceiving for her husband. John was a loose businessman with no ties over on May's end. Josh remained special to May because she fooled a taxi man into thinking that Josh was also his son.

On weekends Josh stayed with May when his adopted parents went to Kingston. This was the time when one of the area taxi men visited and lavished them with money and gifts which rarely seemed to last.

Children four and five were the results of May constantly believing men that they would have taken care of her and her other children. Her sixth and last courtship with Chance produced her baby girl which she was proud of. All of her other courtships produced boys. Chance came from a God-fearing family and she prayed that he would do the right thing and marry her and make her, his wife but her dirty little secret could hinder this.

May met Chance at a church celebration for Grandpa and Grandma's 50th wedding anniversary. His stubborn hair seemed to be tamed into braids that crowned his head. She would usually position herself at the door and wait for him to pass so that she could get the masculine downwind of musk and a tinge of marijuana!

This Baptismal Sunday was no different. She positioned herself into a comfortable nook and waited for him to pass so that she could get her fix. Her thoughts were interrupted by a deep *"hello baby"*!

That Sunday was when the swift courtship began. The long days were spent at work and the chilly nights were spent in each other's arms in the countryside. They enjoyed each other's company. They spoke about their carefree childhood and how they stole fruits from mean farmers. Chance even mentioned one night how he wanted May to become his lawful wife.

May felt her stomach turn over, not only from deception but from her bouts of yet again morning sickness. She remembered when her late Godmother compared her body to that of a rabbit's. May was very fertile and it seemed as if all a man had to do was look at her and she became pregnant.

May lazily dragged her feet at her morning job where she had to clean, wash and iron. Her daily duties were incomplete and the day was almost over. Her thoughts of having to break the news to Chance that she was pregnant were not something that she was happy to share.

She was usually happy to display her swollen stomach. This time it was different not only was she baptized at church and supposed to be reformed but she was secretly sleeping with a pastor's son.

May's walk home was long and she was already tired from her morning job and she still had to go to her night job. She was sure to tell her boss that she would be soon quitting because of her pregnancy and her courtship.

How would Chance react to the news of her prancing around the smoke-filled dance hall where she sometimes did extra favours for more money? She really loved Chance and she wanted to get married to him and settle down.

May decided that after her shift at the club that night that she would sit Chance down and come clean of her double life. May settled in at work and she got lost in the music that was pounding from the speakers, "whine matey whine, whine matey whine"!

True to the fact that May was whining and letting herself go on the stage and making her body tell a story of her appetite. She was even doing The Angel and she even threw in a Dutty Whine and was just about to do a split when she felt a hand pull her off the stage.

It was too dark to see who it was but her gut feeling told her that it was Chance. She could smell the faint musk, and his hands were rough just like Chance's. She was roughly placed into the changing room and that was when she saw Chance's angry yet disappointed face!

Chance questioned her about her intentions with him and in mid-sentence; he walked out as his eyes started to get watery. May felt simple and awful. Chance had previously disclosed all of his secrets to May and thought that she was his soul mate.

May only kept the go-go dancing job so that she could provide for her family. She was tired of depending on men. Even though she also got saved and baptized at church and was supposed to be living a clean life. Her life was far from it!

She continued to go to church and she was hurt to see Chance take another young girl from the area as his wife. Yes, he did try to support their daughter Chantilly. He also shaved his head and was in training to become a lay preacher. So his past lifestyle was now a distant memory.

May's shame was too much to bear so she decided to move to Kingston to help her sister run a mini restaurant that she had just started. May traveled to Town with all of her children and worked hard to support them. She kept no contact with any of her children's fathers and she decided to also depend on God and work hard in her joint business!

THOUGHT FOR THE DAY

Sometimes in life, we think that if we are to compromise our beliefs to make a living for ourselves and our families. How easy it was for May to use her body and get what she wanted. What kind of example did she set for new converts who had a thirst for Christ and who were willing at every instant to share the word of Christ. Many of you, do share the same

interests with the two characters in the story.

Yes, we get excited ladies when a man looks at you the right way and whispers unrighteous things in your ears. Yes, you men who frequent the moonlit stage shows and walk in like Dans and point the gun fingers in the air, fire up the lighters when the Selecta is expected to wheel the tune and come again. Yes, those who do still secretly tap or move their heads when upon hearing a car cruise by with Jah Cure's the latest

"Unconditional love Unconditional love oh oh oh"

When in turn as Pastor gives the sign for the Choir leader to sing a song from the hymnal we go quiet or we just clap.

That same energy was used to chant songs and wave gun fingers in the air to show that you're a bad man. The same fingers that you take to roll your next spliff, or fill a dime bag, those same fingers that steal from your neighbors or molest underage girls, those same hands that open doors to motels and compromise your standings with Christ, those same hands that gamble away and leave pit tans for the continuation of His Church, those same hands that go to area Sister Sarah and Brother Nigel Obeah people and call themselves all kind of spiritual names because they know that you will believe them and dabble in sorcery.

Those same hands that plot to hurt your husbands and wives are the same hands that when we lift them, mean that we are living right. We are being our brother's keeper and holding their hands and lifting them when they fall. We are refraining from our old ways and yes living life anew! Miss May was only one of many fictional characters that went through a lot of the same issues that we battle with. There is good news and it is found in 2 Corinthians 5:17.

It states "Therefore if any man is in Christ, he is a new creature: old things are passed away; behold, all things become new!

ALL I NEED IS YOU

The scene started with Marty Sampson's song:

All I Need is You

*The music started in the background: Left my fear by the side of the road, hear you speak won't let go, fall to my knees, as I lift my hands to Pray......*As the song played, Tracy pulled her knees close to her chest as she tried to let the song overpower her. Her head continued to twitch.

CHORUS PLAYED: *ALL I NEED IS YOU, LORD*

All she wanted was a normal life where she could love and be free....

She roamed around her room and remembered her pastor's voice sounding in her ears reminding her about attending church on the regular, but her daily life was a battle! Some voices constantly plagued her mind and the on and off twitching of her head. She knew that it stemmed from the illicit affair she had had with an African man a few years ago. She was finally at the peak of her daily walk with Christ when she was swept off of her feet by a so-called Christian. He looked the part of a Christian, he spoke the word, but his ancestral ties were not broken. Adding fornication to the list did not help the situation!

Tracy's head was freed momentarily and somehow did not know how her lover's name slipped out of her mouth; she wished that she could be of one mind and not have so many voices. She could not remember the last time she held her bible and was able to read from it. She wished that she could get to church to hear the word of God but even the thought of getting ready would have been a fight. Her head twitched for so many days! On this particular day, her head twitched momentarily and she was able to call out to God!

God was fulfilling his promise, as someone prayed for her and she opened her mouth and uttered His name: Jesus, Jesus, Jesus! She felt her body getting lighter. Her head then twitched for the last time. She blurted out Isaiah chapter 65 verse 24: "Before they call, I will answer while they are still speaking I will hear! For so many days she was unable to call out to God. Her head would shake if anyone came to pray for her. There would be certain voices that would answer the prayer warriors back. At one point in time, it would be Tracy speaking and at another point, it would have been the voice of the enemy masking himself in old ladies' voices, children's voices and so forth.

SONG PLAYING: *ALL I NEED IS YOU, LORD, ALL I NEED IS YOU*

Tracy was now witnessing her body being freed from the spirits of darkness! Both parties were Christians who fell out of the will of God. Like so many of us who are professing Christians and decide that it is time to find a mate and go out of the will of God and have physical relationships where His word clearly states it is a sin. Many of us may have presently escaped the wages of fornication. But the demon-possessed character in the story was not so lucky. She entered into a sexual relationship before marriage against the will of God and it opened her life to the demons living inside her, this caused voices, shifts of reality, and multiple personalities!

During her courtship with this individual, he practiced old traditions that caused him to be still tied to Satan. When Tracy entered into the relationship with that man, she made a pact with the devil; and it opened her wide to the gates of hell. Like Tracy, many have left the throne of grace and have been in a backslidden state. There might be experiences of hardships in life and queries as to what was it that was done and why there is so much suffering? Dear friends, there is a mighty call on your life. For Tracy, it was the demons that plagued her mind. Some might argue that Tracy was suffering from being a schizophrenic, others, multiple personalities, but she was not free! Anyone can become free! The answer is the confession of sins and rededication of life to Jesus Christ! That is the key to life eternal!

Chris Tomlin's song continued to play: *"Lord I Need You"*

"Lord I come

I confess

Bowing here I find my rest

And without you, I fall apart

You're the one that guides my heart

Lord, I need you

Oh, I need you!

Where you are is where I am free

ABOUT THE AUTHOR

Melissa I. Eights-author, educator and toy creator- was born in Aruba and attended St. Thomas University in Miami Florida for her undergraduate and Capella University for advanced studies. Eights enjoys writing, making products and gardening. Among the other books that she has authored, she has also created a skill-based toy of which can be found at www.skilledtraits.com

Grades 8 and up
Fiction
www.skilledtraits.com